THE CHINESE
PUZZLE
BOX

For Ellen and Kerry, short and sweet.

THE CHINESE PUZZLE BOX

MYSTERIES OF ECKERT HOUSE

by CHRIS AUER

smarter · stronger
2:52
deeper · cooler

Zonderkidz

Zonder**kidz**®

The children's group of Zondervan

www.zonderkidz.com

The Chinese Puzzle Box
Copyright © 2005 by Chris Auer
Illustrations Copyright © 2005 by The Zondervan Corporation

Requests for information should be addressed to:
Zonderkidz, Grand Rapids, Michigan 49530

Library of Congress Cataloging-in-Publication Data

Auer, Chris, 1955-
    The Chinese puzzle box / Chris Auer.
        p. cm.–(2:52 mysteries of Eckert House ; bk. 3)
    Summary: Still recovering from his encounter with Rick Doheny, Dan feels someone is
watching him and worries about odd occurrences at the Eckert House museum as he, Pete,
and Shelby work to solve a mystery involving a strange box.
    ISBN 0-310-70872-9 (softcover)
    [1. Puzzles—Fiction. 2. Robbers and outlaws—Fiction. 3. Museums—Fiction. 4. Christian
life—Fiction. 5. Mystery and detective stories.] I. Title.
    PZ7.A9113Ch 2005
    [Fic]–dc22   2004022444

Editor: Amy De Vries
Cover design: Jay Smith–Juicebox Designs
Interior design: Susan Ambs
Art direction: Michelle Lenger and Merit Alderink

Printed in the United States of America

05 06 07 /❖DCI/ 10 9 8 7 6 5 4 3 2 1

CONTENTS

A CURIOUS EVENT

"I think you should stay home. I'd rather you didn't start school next week," said Dr. Steele as she shone a bright light into Dan Pruitt's eyes. "You're still having headaches and that concerns me."

"No school? Well, if you say so," Dan answered a little too quickly.

"Try not to sound so broken up about it," Dan's mother quipped as she looked over the doctor's shoulder.

Dr. Steele made house calls. Freemont, Pennsylvania, was still small enough for that, and besides, twelve-year-old Dan Pruitt was one of her favorite patients.

Dan had made quite a name for himself that summer; he had solved two mysteries, made the local news, the national news, and was profiled in a weekly magazine. Unfortunately, in the process, he received a blow to the head that landed him in the hospital. That injury had given him headaches for the past three weeks and was the reason his doctor wanted him to stay close to home.

Dan waited until the doctor and his mother left before he burst out into hysterical laughter. Missing the first week of school! It was too good to be true.

"Mom, Dan's crying!" yelled one of the Eenies.

"Yeah, he's having some kind of fit," shouted the other one.

Dan's younger sisters, Maureen and Eileen, were seven and eight, rarely apart, and always finished each other's sentences. Dan never called them anything but the Eenies. He jumped up to shut his bedroom door.

"I think I caught something while I was in the hospital," Dan said, clutching his stomach and opening his eyes wide to look crazed. Then he drooled. The Eenies screamed in unison.

"He has rabies!"

"He's contagious!"

They ran shrieking down the hall.

"Dan," his mother called up the stairs.

"Everything's okay up here," he answered innocently.

"Take a nap," she ordered.

"Sure," he said. Dan realized how very tired he really was. It was three o'clock in the afternoon, on a Friday no less. The sun was shining, his skateboard was leaning against the wall, ready to go, but all Dan wanted to do was lie down and sleep. So he did.

The problem with Dan going to sleep at three in the afternoon, was that he woke up at four o'clock in the morning. He had slept for thirteen straight hours, missing his afternoon snack, his dinner, his evening snack, and even the candy bar from his secret stash of junk food. His family always joked about how much Dan could eat.

"We've entered the hollow years," Dan's father had said only a few months before. Dan's father was a Navy flyer and had been stationed overseas for more than three months.

Dan decided to try and sit up. Ever since his injury three weeks ago, sitting up was followed by a throbbing in his skull that took a good minute to stop. Dan waited the usual sixty seconds for the pain to fade. The Langford's dog barked oddly, and he crossed to the window to look out at the street. Hair rose on the back of Dan's neck, and he shivered. There was a part of Dan that was always on edge now, that always felt he was in danger.

When Dan looked out the window, a man was standing on the sidewalk across the street looking up at him. Dan dropped to the floor in terror. It was Rick Doheny, the man who had attacked him! Rick had never been caught.

Breathing heavily, Dan raised himself up ever so slowly on one elbow to peek out.

No one was there.

Dan blinked, rubbed his eyes, and looked again.

"Nice, Pruitt," Dan mumbled to himself. There was a garbage can in the very spot he thought he had seen Rick Doheny. "If someone's dog gets loose, you'll probably see a dinosaur roaming the streets."

Dan reminded himself that although Rick Doheny had not been caught, the police were sure they had spotted him first in St. Louis and then later in Denver. The FBI agent assigned to the case believed Rick was heading toward his cousin in Alaska.

"If only I could believe that," Dan whispered. If he saw Rick Doheny instead of a simple garbage can, then maybe, deep inside, he was more nervous than he thought.

On the way downstairs for his snack, Dan looked in on each of his family members. Neither of the Eenies was under the covers, and the flashlights they used to cast shadow puppets on the ceiling were still on. In the next room Dan's four-year-old brother Jack had a cold and was snoring happily away in his bed.

Down the hall, Grandpa Mike was sleeping soundly, too. Dan's grandfather had suffered a stroke around the same time that Dan's father was shipped overseas. Dan's mother had to take care of her sick father, and that was one of the reasons the family had moved to Freemont. Dan couldn't help but smile as he looked at his sleeping grandfather; Grandpa Mike was doing much better now. He was even learning to speak again.

In her room, Dan's mother had fallen asleep with her laptop computer next to her on the bed. Dan knew that she was keeping a journal of sorts while his father was away.

Dan did a U-turn in the middle of the hall and went back to his bedroom. Seeing his mother's computer made him think of his own letters from his father, and how his dad had asked him to spend some time thinking about a special Bible verse. It was from the Gospel of Luke. Dan grabbed his Bible, went downstairs to the kitchen, and while he was making toast, read the scripture passage. *And Jesus grew in wisdom and stature and in favor with God and men.*

This Bible verse felt a lot like some of the mysteries Dan had solved; Dan knew it was more than just a simple sentence. Right now the word "favor" was what Dan was trying to figure out. He knew that in one sense it meant popularity.

"Jesus was popular when he was a kid?" Dan said aloud, scratching his head. He guessed that made sense. If Dan had been in school with him, he'd have wanted to be his friend. But Dan knew there was more to the word "favor" than popularity. His father had told him so in one of his emails.

Dig a little deeper, Dan, he wrote. *Favor is another word for grace, and there's even an element of mercy involved.*

Grace was another tough word, but Dan knew all about mercy. He had gotten himself into several tight spots that summer, and no one seemed to be holding a grudge. That was mercy.

"Dig deeper," he said aloud as he thought of what his father said. "Deeper," he repeated. Maybe that was the key.

Jesus grew in favor with God . . .

"You really can't do that unless you get closer . . . or deeper . . ." Dan murmured.

So that's what he'd have to do, Dan concluded: spend more time thinking about God.

Dan knew from experience that if he wanted to pull off a certain trick on his skateboard, he had to spend a lot of time thinking about it before he actually tried it; he had to visualize every part of the move first. The more thought he put into it, the more successful he was.

"No reason to think it shouldn't work that way with God," he said.

Of course Dan knew it was one thing to say it, and another to actually do it. He took a large bite of the thickest—and messiest—peanut butter, banana, and marshmallow sandwich he had ever made, and promised that he would try.

A distant rumble of thunder signaled the start of another rainstorm. *Good*, Dan thought. It had been an unusually dry summer until lately. They could really use more rain.

From the backyard, Dan heard the scrape of metal on metal. The garbage cans. Raccoons had become a problem in Freemont. The pesky creatures pried the lids off trash cans and dug through the garbage.

Dan went to the back door to look out. The garbage cans were beside their detached garage, and Dan could make out some movement by the cans. He waited for another rustling sound, then flipped the switch that controlled a floodlight over the garage door. The driveway and backyard went from darkness to light in an instant.

There *was* a raccoon digging through the garbage, but Dan's gaze was riveted on a man standing by Jack's plastic basketball hoop. It was Rick Doheny! This time Dan didn't drop to the floor. He was frozen with fear. A wave of dizziness swept over him and everything went black.

Dan woke up in his own bed. The Eenies were playing a board game on the floor.

"He's awake, Mom."

"He's not drooling!"

Dan's mom hurried into the bedroom. "How are you feeling?"

"Embarrassed," Dan mumbled. He remembered

shouting for the police, the FBI, and the Coast Guard at 4:30 in the morning.

"Don't be. You were just sleepwalking. I got you back into bed."

Dan had a dim memory of looking into the back-yard and seeing . . . what?

"You were pretty upset last night. What was the dream about?"

Rick Doheny. Dan remembered.

"Um, raccoons," Dan answered truthfully. "Big ones."

"And you thought the FBI could help?" his mother quipped.

"Well, you know, if they weren't busy . . ." Dan added with a weak smile. "I'm feeling fine now." Dan swung his legs over the side of the bed.

"Hold on right there," she said, putting her hand against his chest.

"Mom," he pointed out logically, "I've had almost twenty-four hours of sleep and nothing to eat. Plus, it rained again yesterday, so I've been cooped up in this house for like a hundred hours. If I don't get out-side, I'm gonna go nuts. Besides, my head's fine." For the first time since he'd been hurt, when he sat up, his skull didn't pound.

Dan's mother went down to fix him something to eat, and Dan rushed to the Eenies' room at the back of the house. Their window looked out over the backyard. Dan wanted to check for footprints or a sign that someone had been in the backyard the night before. He was too far away to see if there were footprints or not, so he dressed and went down to the kitchen. After gulping down a bowl of soup and practically swallowing his sandwich whole, Dan went out to check the side of the garage. There was an overhang on the roof there, and it was just possible that footprints would not have been washed away that close to the garage.

Dan looked, but found nothing. There were raccoon tracks, but nothing more.

Then, as he was turning to go, something caught his eye. A piece of fabric hung from the fence behind the garage. He carefully lifted it off. It was a red plaid flannel, like from a shirt.

"I don't have a shirt like this," Dan whispered. No one in his family did either.

Think, Pruitt, think, he told himself. Was the man he'd seen last night wearing a red plaid shirt?

Try as he might, he just couldn't remember. He also couldn't remember whether he had ever seen

Rick Doheny wear a shirt with a similar pattern.

"You don't even know if this means anything," he said aloud. But on the possibility that it did, he tucked the piece of fabric into his pocket. Dan knew that whether he liked it or not, he had to pay a visit to Rick Doheny's mother.

If Rick owned a red plaid shirt, she would know. Or, on a scarier note, if Rick was back in Freemont, he might try and see his mother. He might even be staying there. Dan had to find out.

A New Challenge

It was a full week before Dan's mother allowed him to visit Mrs. Doheny. Getting her permission involved approval from Dr. Steele, a clean room, and a promise to be careful.

Mrs. Doheny was a timid little woman in her sixties who had been forced by her son Rick to look the other way while he stole a rare tapestry from Eckert House. Dan biked through Freemont and across the Morgan River to get to her house.

Eckert House, now a museum, had once been the mansion of a

wealthy family whose patriarch had traveled around the world several times. He'd collected everything from rare antiques and valuable artwork, to worthless trinkets and phony masterpieces. After several generations, the Eckert money was gone. The mansion, long in need of repair, was given to the town of Freemont by the last of the Eckerts. It was restored, with many artifacts collected by the family put on display.

Dan worked at Eckert House as a junior handyman. He'd discovered a valuable statue, and now the museum was so popular that visitors needed an appointment to get in. Mrs. Doheny, the woman he was on his way to visit, used to greet those visitors from behind a small desk in the museum's large entrance hall. She quit her job after it was revealed that her son Rick was a criminal. Now she never left her house.

Dan rang Mrs. Doheny's doorbell, worried about her reaction to seeing him again.

"Oh, mercy!" Mrs. Doheny exclaimed when she opened the door. She immediately burst into tears and pulled Dan into a bear hug. It was much tighter and stronger than he would have expected from a woman of her size.

"Hmmff nrg berfng oo," Dan uttered from inside her grasp.

"Mercy, mercy, mercy," Mrs. Doheny repeated through her tears as she pulled Dan into the house.

Five minutes later, Dan sank into the soft cushions of Mrs. Doheny's overstuffed sofa. She had given him a glass of ginger ale, a slice of blueberry pie, three cookies, a piece of fudge the size of a pork chop, and two saltine crackers.

"Eat, eat," she urged him.

Dan was sure that if he ate everything in front of him, he wouldn't be able to stand back up.

"Oh, Daniel, can you ever forgive me for what Rick did to you?" Mrs. Doheny blurted out.

"Mrs. Doheny, it wasn't your fault," Dan said for the twentieth time.

"If I ever see that boy again, I'll turn him over my knee and give him the spanking he should have gotten when he was twelve," she said with real fury.

It was clear to Dan that Mrs. Doheny's anger toward her son was so great that there was no way that she'd hide or protect him in any way. Still, there was the question of the shirt, and Dan tried to think of how to bring it into the conversation.

"You know," he finally said. "My mom is collecting old clothes for some charity or something, so if there's anything you want to give away, now would be a good time."

"What kind of charity?" Mrs. Doheny asked, sounding more interested than he had hoped.

"Beats me," Dan answered. "Probably that homeless shelter."

"That's too bad," she said.

Too bad? Dan was confused. Did she not want the homeless to have clothes? A moment later he understood.

"Before he died, Mr. Doheny gave me a full-length mink coat, but really, how many times do you wear a full-length mink coat?"

"Oh, um, yeah, I hardly ever do," Dan said. Then, realizing how weird that sounded, added, "Not that I have one to wear. But if I did, I wouldn't wear it very often." Dan winced. *Try again, Pruitt*, he told himself. *It's better that she not think you're completely insane.*

"But I had these gloves once," he continued. "Lined with fur. Rabbit's fur, not mink. Way too hot. Drove me crazy. So a full-length mink coat . . . very hot, I'm guessing. Although the homeless do get cold. You never know, they might like it." He stopped.

Maybe if I smile or something she'll think I'm charming, Dan thought. Dan knew he could do charming.

But instead of smiling, Dan laughed. Not a polite little chuckle, but a big hearty — obviously fake — laugh.

"Daniel, are you feeling all right?" Mrs. Doheny asked. She did not look charmed. In fact, she looked scared.

Oops.

"You know, I think I may need to use the bathroom," he said, looking for an excuse to end the conversation.

"Right at the top of the stairs," she said with sudden understanding.

Up in the bathroom a minute later, Dan looked at himself in the mirror. He knew coming here was a very bad idea. He had to pull himself together, march back downstairs, be as polite as possible, and then get out as fast as he could. He splashed some water on his face, and opened the door. As he did, two things happened.

First, he saw an open bedroom door just across the hall. From the sports posters on the wall, he realized it was Rick's room.

Second, the doorbell rang. Mrs. Doheny answered the door, giving Dan an opportunity to check out Rick's room.

The walls of Rick's bedroom were covered with posters of baseball players and surfers. The room was decorated very much like Dan's own.

Why is this bothering me? Dan wondered.

What made one person choose one path and someone else choose another? Friends? Circumstances? Parents?

Maybe I keep seeing Rick when he's not there because I'm worried I'm going to be just like him, Dan thought.

Dan had certainly gotten into a lot of trouble over the summer, and as he lay in the hospital last month he began to understand just how much of it he brought on himself.

"Which is why a deeper relationship with God is a good idea," he mumbled.

Okay, you can play psychiatrist and think about all of this later, Pruitt, he told himself. *Right now look in the closet. See if he has any shirts like the piece of flannel in your pocket.*

Dan opened the closet door. Rick didn't own a lot of clothes, and none of the shirts were either flannel or plaid. Dan breathed a sigh of relief and closed the closet door.

"What are you doing in here?" demanded a voice from the hallway.

Dan's hands shot straight up in the air, and he yelled. He then whirled around to see the one person with whom he could neither pretend nor even try to be charming. Dan was face to face with Miss Alma Louise Stockton LeMay.

Miss Alma was even smaller than Mrs. Doheny. And older. And tougher. And sharper. Dan often joked that if you looked up the word "severe" in the dictionary, you would find Miss Alma's picture there. She was in charge of Eckert House.

"Cat got your tongue, Mr. Pruitt?"

"M-M-Miss Alma," Dan stuttered.

"I'm aware of my name. Are you going to follow it with a sentence?"

Mrs. Doheny appeared behind Miss Alma.

"Mrs. Doheny," Dan said. But again, he stopped.

"I guess you're just naming things," Miss Alma said with an impatient sigh.

"Do you see what I mean?" whispered Mrs. Doheny.

"I'm not crazy," Dan protested.

"That, Mr. Pruitt, is not an opinion you're qualified to give," Miss Alma declared. Fortunately "crazy" kept Miss Alma and Mrs. Doheny from asking him anymore questions about why he was in Rick's room.

Miss Alma then ordered Dan downstairs and into her car. She had come because she needed Dan at Eckert House. Dan's mother had told her where he was. "Just leave your bike here. Your mother said she'd pick it up this afternoon," Miss Alma explained.

Miss Alma drove straight to Eckert House. Once inside, Dan was surprised to see his cousin, Pete, and their best friend, Shelby.

Since he had been hurt, Dan had been spending a lot of time with Pete and Shelby. The relationship among the three of them had changed over the summer, changed in a positive way.

Dan had been pretty embarrassed by his cousin when he first moved to Freemont. Pete and Dan were the same age. Physically, Pete was a lot smaller than Dan. He was also very shy and allowed himself to be pushed around by other kids. Dan didn't allow himself to be pushed around by anybody.

Dan suspected that part of Pete's problem was that Pete was embarrassed by his family situation.

Pete's mother had walked out on Pete and his dad (Dan's Uncle Jeff), and they hadn't heard from her since. Then Pete's dad started to drink and he couldn't hold down a job. It wasn't until recently that everything settled down. Uncle Jeff had stopped drinking, and now he worked as a security guard at Eckert House.

In many ways it was Shelby who smoothed things over between Pete and Dan. If a conversation or a situation between the two cousins got heated, it was Shelby who stepped in and calmed them down. Shelby was the smartest person Dan knew. If there was something she didn't know, she knew where and how to find it out. Dan's nickname for her was Search Engine.

Pete and Shelby were in the Eckert House kitchen. It was off limits to visitors, and the fact that they were sitting there so comfortably surprised Dan. Miss Alma's question surprised him even more.

"Did the pizza arrive yet?"

"In the oven," Shelby answered.

"Real plates, not paper," said Miss Alma, crossing to the cupboard. "I refuse to eat it off a piece of cardboard."

"Who wants a soda?" Pete asked.

In what seemed like ten seconds, the pizza was on the table and the drinks were poured. Dan just stood there stunned. Miss Alma was acting like a human being, and neither Pete nor Shelby seemed to think it was unusual. There could only be one explanation.

"Am I dying?" Dan asked.

"Oh, for pity's sake, sit down. If you were dying, I'd tell you so, Mr. Pruitt."

Now *this* was the Miss Alma that Dan knew.

"You may only open your mouth," she continued, "to take a bite of pizza or sip your beverage."

That was no problem for Dan. He was starving and ate in silence while Pete and Shelby chatted about Pete's cat, Chester.

If Miss Alma was the most feared person in Freemont, Chester was the most feared animal. Chester was twenty pounds of solid muscle. He leaped from treetop to treetop like a squirrel, and lately he had taken to leaping from rooftop to rooftop as well. When a twenty-pound cat, traveling at the speed of sound, lands on a roof, it tends to make anyone inside nervous. It also sets off burglar alarms. The police had responded to calls from terrified citizens convinced that thieves were breaking into their homes from above. Each time it had been Chester.

Chester did have more practical activities, as well. At least Shelby thought so. Reports of raccoon activity in the east part of town were much less than those toward the center of Freemont.

"Which," said Shelby, "lines up exactly with the calls the police received about all those home security alarms Chester set off."

"What's your point?" Dan asked.

"Chester is herding the raccoons," she announced. "I think he's moving them toward the river."

"You mean the way cowboys herd cattle?" Dan was laughing now.

"Why not?" asked Miss Alma. "If that cat were to find a key to a car, I wouldn't be a bit surprised if he started it up and drove it around."

"Sometimes I wake up in the middle of the night and he's at the foot of my bed just staring at me," said Pete. "I know he'd never hurt me, but it's almost like I can hear him saying: 'One false move and they'll find you buried in the kitty litter.'"

Even Miss Alma laughed as she pushed back her chair. "If you're all done, let's go upstairs so I can show you why I wanted to see you today."

"Are you okay?" Shelby asked Dan as they walked up the back stairs to Miss Alma's office on the third floor.

"I'm fine," Dan insisted, quite annoyed.

Miss Alma's office was very small for someone as important to the museum as she was. The phone was ringing as she walked in. It was one of those phones that displayed the number of the person who was calling. When Miss Alma saw who it was, she let out a *humph* and snatched up the receiver. She didn't wait for the person on the other end to speak.

"I got them, they're beautiful, thank you."

She then hung up.

Dan noticed a vase with roses in it on Miss Alma's desk. He nodded to it and elbowed Shelby. Shelby smiled. Miss Alma had a boyfriend. What's more, Shelby, Pete, and Dan had been somewhat responsible for bringing her and Mr. Stoller together.

When Dan first came to work at Eckert House, Miss Alma had given him the diary of a boy whose father was away in Europe fighting in World War Two. She had asked Dan to see if he could figure out the identity of the boy who wrote it.

Dan, Pete, and Shelby wrongly identified Mr. Stoller as the author of the diary. However, their contact with him provided an unexpected result. It turned out that Will Stoller had once tried to court Miss Alma, and he had kept his feelings for her alive for many, many years. He was determined not to let her get away again. He had sent her the roses.

Next to the roses was a cardboard box. Miss Alma opened it, reached in, and took out a model of a small building. It was a miniature Chinese pagoda. Eighteen inches tall, it was made of a dark exotic wood, and each of its three stories was smaller than the one below it. Each roof curved upward at the corners.

"What is it?" Dan asked as he got down on his knees to examine it closely.

"I believe it's a puzzle. A Chinese puzzle box to be exact. And I'd like the three of you to see if you can solve its mystery."

A Further Development

"It doesn't look much like a box," observed Dan.

This was true enough, but the base of the building had a thin, box-like appearance. There was even a little drawer that Miss Alma pulled out. Miss Alma pointed to some faint writing on the edge of the lowest roof. They were Chinese characters. She translated them for Dan, Pete, and Shelby.

"'Apart, together, apart. Treasure within treasure within treasure. Begin your journey.'"

"Okay, everyone who's confused, raise your hand," said Dan.

"Would you like an explanation or would you rather ramble on?"

"An explanation, please," Dan answered meekly.

Miss Alma had an explanation, but in Dan's mind, it raised as many questions as it answered.

"First. Where did I find it? Well, we can thank Rick Doheny for that."

"What? Why?" Dan blurted out. "Did he . . . I mean has he . . . ?"

Miss Alma seemed to know what Dan was trying to say. She answered him gently. "No, Mr. Pruitt, he hasn't been back. This happened before he left. No need to tell you how nosey Rick Doheny was."

Dan let out the breath he'd been holding. What Miss Alma said was true; Rick had explored every inch of Eckert House while no one was looking. He knew all the mansion's secret passageways, undetected doors, concealed staircases, and hidden rooms.

"Well, one afternoon I found him in the attic when I was sure he was in the basement," Miss Alma continued.

Dan nodded. "He used one of the secret passageways to get up there."

"Yes," Miss Alma agreed, "so he could look for things that were none of his business. He made some excuse—as he usually did, and left. After he did, I started looking at what he had found. It was this," she said, indicating the pagoda. "I brought it down here, did some research, and discovered it on a list of items that Julius Eckert brought back with him from China in 1875. There were originally two puzzle boxes; both were given to Jane Eckert who was only ten at the time. I haven't been able to find the other one. It could look like almost anything. This pagoda's an unusual puzzle box, but it's a puzzle box just the same."

"When you say puzzle," Pete said, "what exactly do you mean?"

Miss Alma explained that there were two answers to that question. The pagoda itself was basically a three-dimensional jigsaw puzzle. It came apart in pieces. She demonstrated by pulling out a section of the roof from the second level. She then carefully replaced it.

"If it's already put together, why would we want to take it apart?" Pete asked.

"That's the second answer to your question. If you can put it back together properly, then somewhere on the pagoda, a spring or trigger of some kind is released and a secret compartment is revealed. And then, traditionally, inside that secret compartment is another kind of puzzle. It, in turn, should lead you to some kind of treasure."

Shelby and Pete were carefully examining the pagoda, turning it around, peering through the little windows, checking every little detail. They were much more interested in it than Dan was.

"Miss Alma," Shelby asked, "When we put it back together, is it possible that we might not trigger the secret compartment?"

The answer was yes. Miss Alma obviously did not know just how the puzzle should be reconstructed, but, in her opinion, it was possible that it had to be put back together in a very specific way.

"For example, instead of assembling the first level, and then the second, and then the third, you might need to put the second and third level back together, and then place them as a unit on top of the first level. The release might be triggered by their combined weight."

Shelby asked Miss Alma to give them the translation again. She wrote it down.

"'Apart, together, apart. Treasure within treasure within treasure. Begin your journey,'" Shelby read aloud. "That's a puzzle all by itself. Do you think it will make more sense once we put it back together?"

"I don't know," Miss Alma answered. "That's the mystery."

"It's a puzzle within a puzzle within a puzzle within a puzzle," Pete marveled.

"Give or take a puzzle," mumbled Dan.

An hour later, at a worktable in a small room at the end of the hall, Pete and Shelby had carefully taken the pagoda apart. First, though, at Shelby's suggestion, they had photographed it from all possible angles.

Dan, suddenly exhausted, went to rest on the couch while Pete and Shelby laid out all the pieces. Dan doodled with a pencil. He was not happy. He didn't want another challenge from Miss Alma when he hadn't yet solved the mystery of the diary. Dan talked about it as they sifted through the pieces of the Chinese puzzle box.

Their last efforts to learn the history of the journal had them deciding that notes on a music staff sketched in one of the margins was a clue to the identity of the author. That "clue" had led them to the false conclusion that the diary was Will Stoller's.

Dan was still convinced that the notes were a clue. He opened the diary, which Shelby had brought along. The pattern of six notes, first an E, and then five repetitions of the C above middle C, was just too strange not to mean something. He turned to the page where the music staff was written and sang the sequence of notes for them.

"That's not music," Pete said when Dan was done.

Dan agreed with his cousin. As they had often done in the past, Dan suggested they list what they knew about the diary. "Okay, fact: the entries in the diary start in January of 1943 and end in April of 1945."

"Just before the war ended in Europe," added Shelby.

"Right. From the way he writes, we think the kid was eleven, maybe twelve."

"Our age," nodded Pete. "But we don't know whether or not he actually lived here in Freemont."

"True, but it makes sense that he did since the diary was found here. Fact: the entries are written in ink, but then there are the sketches and the other doodles—like the music notes. Those are done in pencil. And most of them are cartoon characters."

"Except the one," said Shelby. "There's that picture of the airplane."

Dan turned to the entry for January 21, 1945. It was a big plane, possibly a bomber of some sort.

"Oh, good grief," Dan said.

"What's wrong?"

"I'm an idiot! Look at this sketch," Dan said, pointing to the bomber. "What's different about it?"

Pete and Shelby looked. It was quite detailed and fairly large.

"Well," offered Pete, "it looks a lot different than the other drawings in the diary."

"Bingo!" Dan exclaimed. He flipped some pages. "Here, this looks like Mickey Mouse . . . I'm pretty sure this one is Woody Woodpecker. This one back here looks like a guy with a big nose peeking over a fence or a wall . . ."

"What's that mean underneath it?" Pete asked. "I don't get it."

"'Kilroy was here,'" Shelby read. "American soldiers drew that picture and wrote that saying all over Europe after they landed. All around the world, really. Europe, the Pacific Islands, Japan, Korea. It sort of became a contest to be the first soldier to draw it in a new location. GIs hoped to see it when they entered a new town or a new area. It was a reassurance that others had been there ahead of them and everything was all right."

The picture of Kilroy and the words "Kilroy was here" were found several times throughout the diary. Dan showed them another drawing. It was the American eagle with Adolph Hitler in its claw. The style in which it was drawn was also very cartoonish. He flipped back to the picture of the airplane.

"See the difference?" he asked.

"It's more realistic," said Pete.

It was true. Compared to the other sketches, the amount of detail on the plane was amazing.

"And what's interesting is that nowhere else in here has he drawn tanks or machine guns or ships or grenades or anything else dealing with the war. Nothing."

Dan asked Shelby to look at the piece of paper he'd been drawing on while she and Pete were working on the Chinese puzzle box. She picked up the scrap of paper.

"It's an airplane," she said.

"Not just any airplane. It's an F-18. That's the jet my dad flies."

Pete and Shelby looked confused. "We don't get it," Pete finally said.

"The picture is in this diary because it's the plane this guy's father flew during the war. I'm sure of it. It makes sense that he'd have drawn it; it's what *I* draw. I think that if we do some research about the plane, we may figure out who his father was."

"We don't even know what kind of plane it is," Shelby pointed out.

"That's never stopped you before," Pete pointed out.

"Okay, okay," she agreed. "We can figure the airplane part out. Then what?"

"Come with me," Dan said. Three minutes later, Dan, Shelby, and Pete stood in the park across the street from Eckert House. "Then this."

Dan pointed to a monument that they had all seen, walked by, leaned against, and ignored hundreds of times. It was the town's memorial to those in the military that had died serving their country. Those from World War Two were chiseled into the west side of it.

It was difficult for Dan to say what needed to be said because, like the boy from the 1940s, Dan feared for his father's safety.

"Look, that diary just stops cold in April of 1945. The war hadn't ended yet. I don't think his father made it home." Dan stopped. The comparison to his own situation was too painful.

Pete gave Dan a playful punch on the arm. "Your dad's coming back," Pete said.

"Yeah," nodded Dan. "But if the diary was written by someone from Freemont—and my gut tells me it was—then we're looking at the name of that boy's father right now. We just don't know it."

They stood in silence studying the names on the war memorial. They knew there was a sad story behind each and every person listed there.

A few minutes later they were on their way back to Eckert House to not only continue work on the Chinese puzzle box, but having made a renewed decision to crack the mystery of the diary as well.

"You know, Dan, you don't make life easy for us," said Shelby.

"You mean I won't let us give up once we start something? Some people would call that a great character trait. Some people would say that was one of my best qualities."

Pete groaned. "Those people don't really know you."

Pete and Shelby went into the museum ahead of Dan. Dan stopped to look back across the street at the park. A cold stab of fear spread across his chest. Rick Doheny stood behind the war memorial. Dan blinked, for the setting sun was low in the sky. When he looked again, Rick had disappeared, and in his place was an older man walking his dog.

Easy, Pruitt, Dan told himself. *You know he's not there.*

"Coming, Dan?" Shelby called.

Dan stepped into Eckert House and closed the door behind him.

All things considered, Dan was grateful to Miss Alma for giving him the diary and now the other puzzle. He was letting his imagination get the best of him. He thought he had seen Rick just now, and today, the whole time he was sitting in Eckert House, he couldn't shake the feeling that he was being watched. He didn't like that feeling at all.

A DETOUR

There were improvements being made to the security system at Eckert House. One of them was because of Dan.

A thick stone wall surrounded the entire property. It was ten feet tall in most places, but in some spots, it was even higher. A few weeks before, Dan had needed to get over the wall and into the museum. He had done so by using his skateboard, the laws of physics, and a low-hanging tree branch. It had proved to Miss Alma that Eckert House needed more security.

As a result, a wrought iron fence now sat atop the entire stone wall.

It was meant to look decorative and fancy, and it did, but the sharp spikes were dangerous. They served a very definite purpose.

As Dan, Pete, and Shelby climbed the main staircase to the second floor. Dan heard Miss Alma giving Pete's dad a hard time about something.

"As I see it, Miss Alma," Uncle Jeff said, "we have two choices. We can either remove the display, or put some sort of barrier in front of it."

"Why don't we just refuse to admit anyone under the age of twelve?" she answered.

They were in the room filled with children's toys from the 1860s to the 1960s. One display, Jane Eckert's dollhouse, was a replica of the main part of Eckert House before the north and south wings had been added. Even though it was on a high table with a sign that said DO NOT TOUCH, lately children who visited the museum were reaching in and rearranging the furniture.

"Where are their parents?" Miss Alma demanded. "For that matter, where are the security guards?"

Uncle Jeff promised to have someone stationed in the room on a full-time basis when the museum was open since it was the one place where kids seemed to misbehave. Security guards at Eckert

House were becoming more important since it had become so popular with the public. In addition to the regulars, Dan's Uncle Jeff and Tony, there were four other men who rotated shifts. None of them apparently thought the display of toys was that important.

Dan really couldn't blame the kids who played with the dollhouse. He had sneaked in more than a few times to play with some of the windup toys himself. There were cars that went in circles, monkeys that clapped cymbals, dogs that yipped and flipped, helicopters (that really flew), flying saucers (that didn't), fire engines, robots, and monsters. In addition to the windup toys, there were dolls of all kinds and a large model train that circled the room on an elevated track.

Dan, Pete, and Shelby went up to the third floor, but only worked on the Chinese puzzle box for another hour, until the museum closed. Pete and Shelby then left to copy all the names off the war memorial and take them to the VFW to start asking questions. The VFW, or Veterans of Foreign Wars, was an organization of men and women who fought for their country overseas.

Miss Alma told Dan to wait, that she would drive him home when she was done with an important phone call. "It's going to rain again," she said looking out her window at a sky that was clear and sunny. "The last thing you need is pneumonia on top of everything else."

Dan was sure that if he were to point out that the nearest cloud was miles away, Miss Alma would argue that within seconds a storm could sweep in from Canada or Mexico or Antarctica and then where would he be? He decided not to argue. Instead, he used the time Miss Alma needed to wander around the empty museum.

He was halfway down the main staircase on his way to the second floor when he felt it again; the back of his neck tingled.

Dan whirled around, sure that he would catch someone peeking around the corner from above. No one was there. He stood very still. He *knew* someone was there; he knew it beyond a shadow of a doubt.

A minute went by.

Nothing.

He was pretty sure the two security guards, his Uncle Jeff and Tony, were still checking all the doors and windows on the first floor, so it couldn't be either of them. Miss Alma was on the phone with a museum in California; he could hear her just above him.

Then he heard it. It was the soft whisper of a sound. Music. Chimes? No, the gentle plink, plink, plink of a music box.

Daisy, Daisy, give me your answer do . . . Dan sang the words in his head.

There was only one music box in the museum that played that tune, and Dan knew it was locked inside a glass case on the second floor. If someone was in Eckert House who didn't belong there, they were below him.

Dan moved soundlessly the rest of the way to the second floor. The music box was in the room that was once a guest bedroom. It was to the left as Dan came down the stairs, the second door down.

Before Dan had taken half a dozen steps, he heard another sound. It was a kind of whirring. It came from behind him, and he turned quickly to see a little toy car scoot across the hall. It had come from the room that contained all of the toys.

Now what? wondered Dan. Did he go forward to the sound of the music box, which had just stopped playing, or did he double back and investigate the windup car?

The music box could have gone off on its own, he told himself. But the car had to be wound up and then put on the floor. Dan turned and headed back to where the toy had crossed the hall.

Dan stood between the two rooms with a clear view into each. The little car had run into a bookcase and stopped. Looking into the room that contained all the toys, Dan traced an imaginary line to the spot where he thought the car must have been placed. He could see no one in the room. Dan took a deep breath and stepped in.

The moment he entered the room, Dan felt the same sense of being watched that he had felt on the stairs. He shivered as goose bumps spread up his arms.

"The museum is closed," he said aloud. He took another step into the room. Then another. "Did you hear me?" But he could see from where he stood that no one else was there.

Okay, Pruitt, go over the possibilities, he ordered himself. There was usually a logical explanation for everything. Only what was logical about an old toy jumping down from a shelf and going for a ride?

The most likely explanation, Dan decided, was that someone had wound it earlier, and then put it down. For whatever reason, the spring didn't release, and the car didn't move. Then a vibration, maybe from the air conditioning, maybe from a door being closed, jogged it loose, and off it went. Zip. Perfectly logical.

And I don't believe it for a moment, Dan said to himself. Both Miss Alma and his uncle were in this room earlier, and for the car to travel the way it did, it would have to come from . . .

"There," he said out loud. He was looking at a spot on the far side of the room. A spot Miss Alma would have seen if the car had been there then. It was a straight shot right out the door, across the hall and into the other room. He walked over to the wall.

"What are you looking for, Pruitt?" he asked. He already knew. He was looking for something that might conceal yet another hidden passageway, one he had not yet discovered. A place for someone to step out, wind the car, then disappear again.

He ran his hands up and down the wall, looking for some kind of seam or bump or crack. He found what might be a seam.

Another minute of exploring and Dan found a small bump on the molding near the floor. It looked like the head of a nail that had been painted over, and Dan almost missed it. He jiggled it, and a second later he was rewarded with the sound of a click and the creak of a door swinging open.

The opening was thin, maybe only two feet wide, and it was only about four feet high. Dan would have to stoop to get inside.

The last thing he wanted to do was explore the dark passageway without a flashlight. He scanned the room for something he could use. On a shelf was a flashlight from the 1950s, shaped like a rocket ship.

I don't suppose anyone put batteries in it, Dan thought. But they had. Miss Alma was very efficient.

Dan turned the flashlight on and stepped into the darkness. Eckert House was full of secret passageways and staircases, but Dan had never been in this one, he was sure of that.

In the past, Dan would have walked into the space without a second thought. He knew better now. He had gotten stuck in a passage before. He needed something to keep the door from closing all the way. He grabbed a teddy bear and wedged it into the door frame so the secret panel wouldn't close and lock him in. That done, he inched forward.

Instinct told Dan to go right. Right was toward the main staircase.

Dan used the flashlight to examine the walls and the floor. He didn't want any surprises.

After about thirty feet or so, he stopped when he heard a noise, a kind of bump followed by several creaks. It was right above him. Dan quickly directed his flashlight to a spot over his head. The noise stopped. Dan was sure that there was another concealed passageway just above him, and he felt just as sure that someone was up there.

Dan held his breath and didn't move. He listened carefully for some sign, some noise, something that would tell him he was right. When he heard another creak, he realized he needed to get back out into the toy display room. And fast.

About halfway back to the opening, Dan's flashlight swept across something on the wall. He stopped. It was a picture, a familiar picture, a picture he and Shelby and Pete had discussed just that afternoon. It was a man with a big nose looking over a fence. But instead of saying "Kilroy Was Here" it said "I Was Here."

Dan's stomach tightened. The picture and the lettering looked new, as if they had been drawn recently. The ink looked wet.

Maybe it's just a trick of the light, he told himself. This "Kilroy" didn't have to be new. It could have been there since the 1940s.

But whoever put it here had used a felt-tipped marker of some kind, and even if felt-tipped markers were around during World War Two—and Dan suspected they weren't—then certainly the ink would be dull and faded, not dark and shiny as this was.

"I was meant to find this," Dan whispered. Then, as he reached to touch the drawing to see if the ink was still moist, he heard a scream. It was Miss Alma.

Dan scrambled out of the passageway and pulled the panel shut behind him.

Miss Alma screamed again. Dan ran out into the hall and joined Uncle Jeff who was running up the staircase. Together they raced to the third floor.

A Rat's Nest

"Rats!" screamed Miss Alma. "At least four of them!"

Miss Alma was standing on a chair and pointing a gun at something in the corner.

"Miss Alma, you can't just shoot them," Uncle Jeff shouted.

"It's not a gun, it's a lighter," she shouted back. "The rats don't know the difference. If I had a real gun, I most certainly would shoot them. In fact, give me yours," she ordered Uncle Jeff.

Uncle Jeff convinced Miss Alma that blasting away at the rats (which had wisely disappeared) was not the safest choice. "Call an exterminator instead," he suggested.

Uncle Jeff headed down to the kitchen where he was sure there were some old mousetraps. Miss Alma told Dan to help his uncle.

Dan hurried away, suddenly realizing that the presence of rats in the museum explained a lot.

The dollhouse, for example. Rats could have been responsible for the mess. They might also have been responsible for the noises. He could hear a scurrying sound in the walls. These particular rats were quite loud. Of course, if he were fleeing from Miss Alma, he'd probably be loud himself.

Then there was the matter of the windup toy. A rat *could* have knocked it over and set it off.

And a rat could have been behind him when he was on the stairs and felt sure he was being watched. Actually, any of the times he felt he was being watched, it could have been the rats.

"Even the music box could have been started by one of them nosing around," he said.

But Dan realized even as he said it that he *hoped* it was true more than he *believed* it was true. The problem was the picture of Kilroy behind the wall. That was just too weird. And too much of a coincidence.

Dan had to get back inside and take a closer look. But not now. Now he had to help Miss Alma and Uncle Jeff.

Uncle Jeff was laughing when Dan entered the kitchen. "Miss Alma's afraid of rats," he said.

"I'm not too wild about them either," Dan offered.

"Yeah, but about the best that was going to happen with that lighter was to offer them cigarettes and hope they'd smoke themselves to death."

Dan commented that he thought it was odd that the rats would just suddenly appear the way they did. Uncle Jeff thought it was because of all the rain they'd had lately, that some of their normal nesting places had flooded out.

"Hey, what about Chester?" asked Dan.

"What about him?"

"Why couldn't we slip him into Eckert House? It'd be rat-free in less than twenty-four hours."

"Tell you what," said Uncle Jeff. "If you can get him in here, go for it. But leave me out of it. That cat's getting very strange. The other day I found him wearing a coonskin hat."

There were only ten mousetraps, so Dan and his uncle set them at strategic places around the museum. While doing this, Dan saw one of the rats.

It took him by surprise. Not that he saw a rat, for he almost expected it. What surprised Dan was the rat's color. It was pure white.

"What color were the rats you saw?" he asked Miss Alma a little later.

"They were rat-colored," she snapped. "What kind of question is that?"

Dan dropped the subject. But a white rat seemed very odd to him.

That night Shelby and Pete stopped by Dan's house. They brought Mr. Stoller with them.

For a man who had spent almost fifty years refusing to come out of his house, the past few weeks had been quite a change for Will Stoller. He was now seen all over Freemont, and many of those who had known him as a young man were glad to get to know him all over again.

Much of the change in Will Stoller's personality had to do with the Eenies. They pestered him every day, but Will didn't seem to mind at all. In fact, just the opposite. He had already been bike riding, rowing on the river, and knew how to turn on a computer and surf the Net. The Eenies had seen two movies starring their new favorite actor, Cary Grant, learned to dance the jitterbug, and had discovered a book about some kid named Tom Sawyer. The three of them were quite a team.

Will wore a suit and a snappy bow tie.

"Looking sharp there, Mr. S.," one of the Eenies said.

"Going sparking?" said the other.

"That's enough, ladies," their mother said.

But they didn't stop until they learned that Will was taking Miss Alma to the dance at the VFW Hall.

"VFW?" asked Dan. "As in—?"

"Veterans of Foreign Wars," answered Shelby.

That's when the whole story came out. Shelby and Pete had gone to see Will when they left Eckert House. Since his brother's name was on the War Memorial in the park, they figured he might know some of the other families who had lost loved ones in the war.

"I stopped talking to just about everyone after the war, so the answer to their question was no," Will added. "But I figured it was time I got to know some of those good folks. So I made a few phone calls."

During one of those calls he learned of the dance, so he made one more call, to Miss Alma.

"I told her she had driven you kids crazy by giving you that diary, and the least she could do was accompany me to the dance tonight to ask some questions and help you out."

So off to the dance they were going, although Miss Alma insisted it wasn't a date.

"She's calling it research," said Will with a wink. "Of course you can call a horse a camel if you want, but if it wins the Kentucky Derby, then I say give it a bucket of oats and call it a day."

Dan thanked Will for his help, and the Eenies walked him out to his car.

Pete and Shelby also brought other news.

"Okay," said Shelby, "you were right. That plane drawn in the diary was easy to identify. It's a B-24. Its nickname was The Liberator."

"It was flown mostly in Europe," Pete added. "The Eighth Air Force. We told Mr. Stoller all about it, and he's going to keep that in mind when he's asking questions tonight."

"I think we've got a decent chance of solving this mystery," Shelby concluded.

Dan was pleased. He told them what had happened with the rats after they left, and to his relief, both Pete and Shelby felt that they, too, were being watched that afternoon. They didn't have any problem blaming the rats.

"Creepy," said Pete with disgust.

Dan then told them about the Kilroy sketch inside the wall. Neither Pete nor Shelby seemed to think it was important. It would have been the perfect time for Dan to tell them about "seeing" Rick Doheny, and his fear that he was back. But he already knew what they'd say: that seeing Rick and imagining that Rick was in Eckert House was a result of the bump on his head.

Later that night, Dan addressed that in his prayers.

"Please, God, help me to make better choices than Rick did. And please take this fear away."

When Dan finished the "formal" part of his prayers, he lay very still, listening. An occasional flash of lightning — still many miles away — made a weak, flickering light in his room. He heard no thunder.

This "listening prayer" was something new to Dan. He was giving God a few minutes of silence. It was something his father had recommended in a letter that arrived that day.

See if you can be still in God's presence when you pray each day, Dan. Interesting things can happen. He's been known to say an important thing or two from

time to time. Think of Abraham . . . think of Noah . . .
Be still and listen.

Dan figured this was part of what his father meant about going deeper with God. So, silence it was.

Dan was not good at silence.

First his mind went over everything Pete and Shelby had shared with him earlier that night. Then he went back to the events at Eckert House, then . . .

"Stop," he said aloud.

Dan decided to concentrate on images. Maybe that would help.

Images it was. Things that reminded him of God, things like waves crashing on a beach, steep rocky cliffs that plunged into cold mountain lakes, sunlight sparkling on water . . .

Dan felt himself relax. He was no longer forming words in his head. It was nice.

Then it happened. A thought. The words were not his.

Sometimes fear is really a warning.

Dan sat up in bed, breathing hard. His heart was racing.

But I don't want to be afraid, he said to himself. I'm not supposed to be afraid.

Maybe this isn't fear. Maybe it's a warning.

"That's you talking, Pruitt, not God," he said aloud.
Even so, it was after midnight before he fell asleep.

A FEW
SURPRISES

The next day was Sunday, and Eckert House was closed. Unfortunately, because it was Sunday, Miss Alma could not get an exterminator to come and deal with the rats. That meant Eckert House would have to be closed on Monday as well.

Dan, Pete, and Shelby met Miss Alma and Will Stoller coming out of church.

"How did it go last night?" Shelby asked.

"Fantastic," Will declared. "We danced every dance and closed the place down."

"Your next sentence will be your last if I am in it in any way," warned Miss Alma.

Will gave them a wink and reported that there were some promising leads. "Give me a few more days," he said.

"I don't suppose I could interest the three of you in a safari of sorts?" Miss Alma asked in an obvious attempt to change the subject.

The "safari" was a trip to the museum to empty the traps, set new ones, and deal with whatever chaos the rats had caused. Dan, Pete, and Shelby agreed to go at once.

It was strange going into the museum that afternoon. Dan had been there alone several times and had all the exhibits to himself. But to walk in knowing that little animals were watching them was, to put it mildly, creepy.

There was a new security guard on duty, a pleasant man named Roger. He knew from Alma that Dan and the others were coming and let them in. Before stepping inside, Pete left a small paper bag near the door.

"What's that?" Dan asked.

"Chester's favorite snack." Pete nudged the sack with his toe. "If he smells it, then he'll come looking for it. And if he comes looking for it, then he'll eat it. And if he stands here and eats it, then he'll smell the rats, and if he smells the rats, then he'll find a way to get inside. And if he gets inside . . ."

"Then it's good-bye, rats," finished Dan. "Have you also considered that it's 'good-bye, people' once he finishes off the rats?"

When they questioned Roger, they learned that the rats had made considerable noise throughout the night, but that, so far, he had not seen any. Dan, Pete, and Shelby left to check the traps. Their first surprise that afternoon was to find all the traps empty.

"The bait's gone," observed Dan. "All the traps have been sprung, but no dead rats." Since a mouse-trap makes a loud snap when it is set off, they asked Roger if he had heard anything.

"Sorry, kids," he said with a shake of his head. "I'm as confused as you are." He returned to his post in the security office.

They carefully reset all the traps and added others that they had brought with them.

"Now what?" asked Pete when they were finished.

"Now we wait. And while we do," Dan said, lowering his voice, "let me show you what I found yesterday."

When they entered the exhibit room with all the toys, they got their second surprise of the day. Many of the toys around the room were knocked over. The dollhouse, the one modeled after Eckert House, was a total wreck. The furniture inside was scattered, and some pieces were even broken.

"These must be some really big rats," said Shelby.

Dan called to Roger, who joined them a minute later. He, too, was surprised by what he saw. When Dan asked about the last time he looked in on the room, Roger was sure that it was during his six a.m. rounds.

"Did you actually step inside the room, or did you just stand at the door and look around?" asked Dan.

Roger was sure he had stepped in. And that the toys had not been disturbed. "I wouldn't miss something like that," he said.

Dan didn't want to be rude, but it was almost three in the afternoon. He was surprised that Roger hadn't been in the room since so much earlier in the day.

"Well," explained Roger, "Kevin did the next set of rounds. At eleven. But he went home sick just before you got here. He didn't say anything to me about this room, but I can find out." He left to make the phone call.

The third surprise of the day came a few moments later. Dan pulled out a small flashlight he'd brought along and knelt beside the spot that had triggered the secret panel.

"We only have a minute," he said. "I want you to at least see what I saw." He jiggled the little bump that had opened the door for him the day before. Nothing happened. He tried again. Still nothing. He ran his hands across the wall. Did he have the right spot? Was there another bump somewhere? There wasn't.

"This has to be it," he muttered. But no matter what Dan did, he couldn't get the switch to work. He saw Pete and Shelby exchange a nervous glance. "I'm not crazy," Dan said forcefully.

"I believe you," Shelby replied. "And I believe that the 'Kilroy' sketch is inside that wall. You'll just have to find another way to get inside."

"But this switch *did* work," insisted Dan.

"Okay." Shelby shrugged, indicating it was no big deal. "Now let's put this room back the way it's supposed to be." She went to set the furniture straight within the dollhouse, leading to the fourth surprise of the day. "Dan, how well do you know this dollhouse?"

Shelby pointed out that it appeared to be put together in sections rather than in one solid piece. There was a spot between the main hallway and the library that had a gap in the wall. There was another between the main bedroom on the second floor and the little sitting room next door.

"I think each room can be pulled out separately," she said.

"Is that unusual?" Dan asked.

She explained that a dollhouse was usually put together like a regular house: first the outside walls, then the first floor, second floor, and so on. To test her theory, she carefully pulled on the second floor sitting room. It slid out an inch or so, much as a drawer would slide out of a dresser.

"Weird," she murmured.

Just then, Roger returned with the news that Kevin had gotten sick while making his rounds. He never made it to the second floor. The rats had done their mischief sometime between six in the morning and three in the afternoon. Roger left again to answer the telephone.

Shelby pulled on Dan's sleeve. "Lean down. What does this dollhouse remind you of?" she asked, pulling the dining room out a few inches, and then replacing it.

"The pagoda," Dan cried. "It's even made of the same kind of wood!"

"Could this be the other puzzle box? Both were for Jane Eckert, and both were given to her in 1875," Shelby said.

"Miss Alma wouldn't miss something like that," offered Pete.

"Let's get the Chinese puzzle box together and see if there's a connection," Dan called, heading up to the third floor. Pete and Shelby followed.

When they walked into the workroom where they had been assembling the puzzle, they were surprised to find the pagoda almost completely assembled. It was obvious where the last few pieces were to be placed.

"Uh, Dan, did you do this after we left yesterday?" asked Pete.

"I didn't touch it."

"We only assemled the first level," Shelby said. "We separated the pieces that belonged to the second and the third stories, but that was it."

"Does it look right?" Dan asked.

Pete and Shelby thought that it did.

It was decided that Kevin, the security guard who went home sick, was the likely culprit. Miss Alma was also considered.

"It really doesn't make any difference," Shelby decided. "Let's just finish it and see what we have."

They did. It took about an hour because they ran into a couple problems. As the enormous clock down in the entrance hall chimed that it was four thirty, Dan placed the third level of the little pagoda onto the second level. As he did, there was a soft click. A section on the second floor of the little model sprang open.

Inside was a small piece of paper with writing on it.

A PUZZLE WITHIN A PUZZLE

Dan slowly lifted the thin sheet of paper from its resting place within the compartment of the Chinese puzzle box. A powerful thunderstorm which had been gathering for some time made the room very dark. Pete switched on the lamp.

"'Together, apart, together,'" he read. "'Within duplicate walls lies a treasure of the greatest worth. Seek it. Acquire it. Never lose it. A little touch, seeker within a larger touch, seeker. Finish the journey.'" It was signed Julius Eckert.

The three friends were silent. The confusing words seemed to hang in the air. They studied the pagoda. They copied the words on another piece of paper in case something happened to the original message. It was Dan who finally spoke.

"Let's start with the first part. 'Together, apart, together.' Which is the opposite of what's written on the puzzle itself. 'Apart, together, apart.' When we found it, it was together, right? So we took it apart and put it back together again."

"Which got us the second message," said Shelby, laying the one they had written out next to the assembled puzzle. "'Together, apart, together,'" she read.

"Do you think we're supposed to take the pagoda apart again?" Pete asked. "Or do you think it means the other puzzle box?"

They decided either was possible, but thought it best to try and figure out the rest of the message first.

"We're definitely talking about another treasure here," Dan stated. "I'm sure the words 'duplicate walls' mean one of the secret passageways in Eckert House." He didn't have to remind them that a valuable tapestry was hidden inside one of the walls for years before it was discovered just a few weeks ago.

"How do we know the treasure doesn't mean that tapestry?" asked Pete.

"Follow me." Dan ran out of the room and down the hall to Miss Alma's office. Pete and Shelby followed.

There was a file folder on Miss Alma's desk marked "K.T." It stood for the Kellenberg Tapestry. This was the hidden tapestry that had disappeared along with Rick Doheny. Dan opened the folder and read from it.

"Purchased from an Austrian Baroness in 1883." He closed the folder. Neither Pete nor Shelby seemed to get his point. "The puzzle box was brought here in 1875—long before 1883. Remember? Miss Alma told us yesterday. Which means there is another treasure inside these walls."

"But Dan," Shelby objected.

Dan wouldn't let her finish. "'A little touch, seeker,'" he quoted from the clue. "What does that sound like?" Dan answered for them. "It's an instruction for us, the seekers, to open a secret passageway like the one I found yesterday. You touch it gently, and bingo, a door opens." Dan felt the phrase "within duplicate walls" also supported this.

Pete and Shelby agreed that this was possible. But Shelby had a problem with that very sentence in the clue.

"'A little touch, seeker within a larger touch, seeker,'" she quoted. "It's such an odd phrase. The language doesn't seem right. It doesn't fit with the rest of the clue."

Dan shrugged. "First, it was written in 1875, so I'd expect it to sound strange. And second, I think that's the important sentence so the puzzle maker wanted it to be different."

Pete frowned. "Let's say you're right. What is 'the larger touch, seeker' supposed to mean?"

"I have no idea. I think once we get inside the wall that the second part of the riddle will make more sense."

Dan's best guess, using the clue, was that the wall was together, it had to come apart, and then, once they were inside, two things — whatever they were — had to come together again.

"The question is, which wall?" he asked.

A loud clap of thunder announced that the gathering storm was finally upon them. The rain fell so hard that Dan couldn't see more than fifty feet beyond the house.

"It looks like I got here just in time," a familiar voice said behind them. It was Miss Alma. "Are we winning the war against the rodent population? Do you need reinforcements? And what are you doing in my office?"

Dan, Pete, and Shelby came away from the window and brought her up to date on the rats.

"I suggest you make the rounds of the traps again." Miss Alma glanced the trap in her office. "That empty trap does *not* make me happy," she added.

None of the other traps had been sprung either.

When they returned from checking, Dan was surprised to find Pete's dad talking to Miss Alma. "Hey, Uncle Jeff, I didn't know you were working today."

"I wasn't supposed to," he answered.

The reason was not pleasant. Roger, the other security guard, had called him twenty minutes ago to come in. Roger was downstairs in the security office with a violent headache that was making him sick to his stomach. Uncle Jeff asked Miss Alma to come down and look at Roger.

She grabbed an umbrella as she left the office.

"Are you going outside?" Dan asked.

"No, I am not," she answered sharply.

"I think it's for the rats," whispered Uncle Jeff.

Dan, Pete, and Shelby went back to the workroom where they had assembled the puzzle. They studied the message again, but no new interpretations occurred to them.

"Guys, my dad looked really worried," Pete said. "I'm gonna go see if there's something I can do to help."

Dan thought this was a good idea. "If all three of us go down, it would probably irritate Miss Alma." After Pete left, Dan turned the assembled puzzle box around and around.

"You'd think there'd be some clue about where we should start looking," he said. "I mean, really, maybe kids were smarter back in 1875, but Miss Alma said that Jane Eckert was only ten when she was given . . ." Dan stopped.

"What?" asked Shelby.

"Where would a kid play with a puzzle?" Dan asked.

"In her room!"

"It could still be there, maybe in a hidden passage! Which of these rooms was Jane Eckert's when she lived here?"

The only way to find the answer to that question (without bothering Miss Alma) was to look at the photographs and sketches in the library that told the history of the house. Hopefully one of them would have that information.

A few minutes later, they found an old photograph of Jane Eckert at a dressing table in a long white dress. It was a very artistic pose. The photograph was dated 1883.

"She would have been eighteen," Shelby said.

"Look in the mirror," Dan said. "Look at the upper corner." He pointed to a window reflected in the mirror.

"When we find this window, we find Jane Eckert's bedroom," Dan declared.

The second floor seemed the logical place to start. Most of the family bedrooms had been there when the Eckerts lived in the mansion. Dan and Shelby went from room to room and checked every window. Nothing matched the photograph. At one point, Shelby rounded the corner and headed into the north wing. Dan stopped her.

"The north and south wings weren't added until later," he reminded her.

Then, in a third floor room, they found the window that matched the one in the photograph. The room was once Jane Eckert's bedroom.

None of the rooms on the third floor of the museum was open to the public, and most, like this one, were used for storage. It was next to Miss Alma's office. However, there was a problem. Permanent shelves had been built against every wall. Dan went to each shelf and pulled on it.

"What are you doing?" asked Shelby, alarmed.

"I can't believe they did this!" he cried. "Are they all nailed to the wall?"

They were.

"How are we going to get into any secret passages?"

"Look," Shelby reminded him, "we don't know that we're right about any of this."

"*I* do," insisted Dan. Once again, he circled the room, pulling on the shelving.

"But we've had the clue less than an hour! There could be a dozen different solutions, stuff we haven't even thought of yet!" Shelby took a deep breath. "Listen. It could be a lot deeper or more complicated than a secret passageway or the kind of treasure you think it is."

Deeper. That word stopped Dan.

Deeper. He connected it to the stillness and the quiet he tried during his prayer the night before.

Deeper. Slow down, Pruitt, he told himself. And listen. You don't listen enough. You can't get closer to the truth—any kind of truth—if you don't listen.

Dan shivered.

"Are you all right?" asked Shelby, patting his arm.

"No," Dan answered truthfully. For suddenly he could not ignore that still, small voice he heard in his prayers last night, the voice that said his fear could be a warning. "Something's wrong," he added.

"What?" whispered Shelby. She sounded scared.

I don't know. It's like I'm supposed to add one plus one and get three, and all I have to do is write the answer down, only I just can't bring myself to do it." He stopped. "Something's wrong," he repeated.

Dan told Shelby everything. He told her about seeing Rick Doheny, about the piece of cloth he found on the fence, and about standing in Rick's bedroom and being worried that he and Rick were similar. He told her about not being able to shake the feeling that he was being watched—and not just by rats. He told her about his sincere belief that he and Pete and Shelby were overheard yesterday, and that the "Kilroy" in the wall was not a coincidence. He even mentioned his prayer and the warning he felt he heard.

Shelby listened without interruption. When Dan finished, she insisted they head downstairs to tell Miss Alma.

"You don't think I'm crazy?" he asked.

"I think you should have told us this yesterday," she answered.

Dan and Shelby walked out into the hall. The thunderstorm was still raging outside. Suddenly the lights flickered and went out.

"Wait a minute, it's *too* dark," Dan said.

"I guess we lost the electricity," Shelby answered.

"It's more than that." Dan looked up at the ceiling.

At each end of the hall was an emergency set of lights that automatically went on when the power went off. They were connected to the generator that also kept the museum's alarm system up and running, no matter what. The emergency lights— and thus the alarm system too—were off.

"We have a very big problem," Dan whispered.

A Near
Miss

Dan pulled out his flashlight, and he and Shelby raced to the first floor. As they did, they noticed the sound of the wind and the rain as it beat against Eckert House. Dan had never heard or seen anything quite like it. It was only six o'clock, but it seemed as dark outside as if it were midnight. A loud crack from the side of the house caused them both to jump.

"What was that?" Shelby cried.

"Tree branch," was Dan's brief answer.

A gust of wind rattled the two massive front doors, which were ajar, and Dan slammed them shut.

They heard Miss Alma call out from the back of the building.

"Hello! Anybody?"

The security office was near the end of the hall that led to the kitchen. When Dan and Shelby got there, they found Miss Alma with Roger. Roger was slumped in a chair with his head in his hands. Miss Alma was applying a wet cloth to his neck. There were no windows in the small room that had once served the mansion as a pantry, so Miss Alma had switched on Roger's flashlight and rested it on the edge of the desk.

"Where have you been?" Miss Alma cried. "I need your help. Fast." She went on to explain that not only was the electricity out, but the phone lines were down. Roger was very sick and needed a doctor. To make matters worse, Dan's Uncle Jeff was beginning to get sick as well. He had gone down to the basement to see if he could get the emergency power on, but had not returned. "Shelby, go to my office and get my cell phone. It's in my purse. Dan, go down and check on your uncle," she finished. She made sure each of them had a flashlight and urged them to hurry.

Back out in the hall, Dan stopped Shelby before she headed up to the third floor.

"Are you gonna be okay?" he asked.

"Hey, no phones, no power, no security system, the guys who are supposed to protect us are sick, if we step outside we'll end up in Oz, and there are rats swarming to attack us. What's there to worry about?" she said.

Dan smiled. "Just another boring day." He opened the door to head down to the basement. "See you in a few," he tossed over his shoulder before disappearing into the darkness.

There was a turn in the stairs about halfway down to the basement, and Dan could see the light from his uncle's flashlight on the wall. When Dan rounded the corner, though, he found his uncle seated on the floor with his head in his hands.

"Glad you're here," Uncle Jeff mumbled. "Very sick . . ."

Dan knelt next to him. "What can I do to help?"

"We're in trouble, Dan . . . the circuit breaker is fried." He indicated the panel above him with a nod of his head.

Dan directed his flashlight up. He knew almost nothing about electrical circuits or wiring, but one look at the board told him enough. It was smoking and covered with scorch marks. It had to be a direct hit from lightning.

Dan helped his uncle to his feet.

"First Kevin, then Roger, now me. Something's wrong, Dan. This isn't the flu. Maybe some kind of chemical leak . . . insecticide . . . If I didn't know any better . . ." Uncle Jeff did not finish. He gripped his stomach as a wave of nausea swept over him.

Something about his tone alarmed Dan. "If you didn't know any better, what, Uncle Jeff? Do you think you were poisoned?"

Uncle Jeff nodded. "It's possible."

Dan got his uncle back to the security station and found out that Miss Alma's cell phone was not in her purse.

"I don't understand," Miss Alma exclaimed. "I know for a fact I put it in there. I'll have to drive them to the hospital myself." She stood up, then sat right back down. "I can't! I'm parked inside the electric gate." She told Dan he would have to go out into the storm and open it manually.

She walked Dan to the front door, leaving Shelby to watch over the two sick men. Miss Alma being Miss

Alma, she kept giving Dan instructions. Suddenly she stopped.

They were in the entrance hall, and she looked up the main staircase. Dan knew better than to ask her what was wrong. "Where's Pete?" she finally asked.

"Pete! I don't know!" When was the last time Dan had seen Pete? Did he come downstairs with him? No, it was before that. A long time before that. "You went down to check on Roger, and then his dad went down too, and Pete was worried, so he . . ." Dan swallowed hard. "Miss Alma, it's been over an hour since I saw him."

Miss Alma patted him on the shoulder. "Well, we know he didn't leave. You go and get help, and I'll look for Pete. And I don't want puddles all over these floors when you get back."

Dan's errand was more urgent than ever. Even though Miss Alma tried to make light of Pete's absence, Dan saw the same thing in her eyes that he was sure was in his own: gut-wrenching fear.

The wind was so strong that the rain was blowing sideways. Dan ducked his head and made his way down the wide front steps and out into the open. The rain stung his face. It hurt, and when he held out his hand he noticed tiny pellets of hail.

Dan took a few careful steps along the slippery brick walk. Then a gust of wind hit him that was so strong it knocked him down onto the grass.

"That was graceful," Dan said aloud. He struggled to his feet.

A large limb from one of the maple trees lay across a section of the lawn and over part of the walkway. As Dan walked toward it, he noticed a patch of gray fur concealed within the leaves.

"Chester!" Dan called out.

Dan never knew what to expect with Chester, and he certainly wasn't expecting an affectionate greeting complete with purring and an appreciative rub against his leg. On the other hand, he wasn't expecting what he got, either. Chester leaped out and hissed at Dan. Dan jumped backward.

"Are you scared, buddy?" he asked. Stupid question, Dan said to himself. Chester feared nothing. "Pete left you a nice treat on the porch. And if you're still hungry after that, there's about four or five hundred rats inside."

Chester arched his back and hissed again. He was ready to attack and Dan knew it. This was not going to be pretty.

Then a remarkable thing happened. A raccoon that Chester had cornered took his one chance at freedom and made a break for the wall. Rather than pursue it, Chester just looked over his shoulder, then looked back at Dan and hissed again.

"You'd rather eat me than a big, fat, juicy raccoon?" Dan asked in disbelief.

A second later, Dan jumped in real terror, for the raccoon, upon reaching the stone wall and not finding a way up, scurried to the iron gate. As soon as it touched the metal there was a loud crack and a flash of light. The raccoon was thrown back and lay dead on the ground.

Dan couldn't believe it. The raccoon had been electrocuted.

But how?

Dan quickly scanned the yard. He didn't see the electrical lines at first; the rain was coming down hard and there were so many broken branches and scattered leaves that they were mostly covered up. But about a hundred feet north, a high voltage wire had been knocked down by the storm. It was touching the newly installed iron fence that stood atop the stone wall surrounding the entire property.

The fence had to be charged with thousands of volts of electricity. Dan guessed that this was the reason all the electrical systems in the museum had been destroyed; somehow the power had surged inside and taken out all the circuits.

Circuits. Dan didn't know a lot about electricity, but he remembered an experiment from fourth grade. An electrical current would flow through wires if the wires were unbroken. He looked left and right, knowing that the iron fence through which all that electricity was flowing was an unbroken circuit around the entire property. Dan knew that if he were to even brush against it, he would end up like the raccoon. *They were all trapped inside Eckert House.*

Chester meowed at Dan's feet. The cat had actually saved his life. Dan took a chance and leaned down to pet him. Chester rubbed his wet head against Dan's hand and meowed again.

"You, my insane cat friend, have just earned yourself the biggest piece of fish I can find at the supermarket. Thanks." Then, remembering who was really behind his safety, Dan closed his eyes and said a quick thank you to God.

Dan made his way through the blinding rain back to the house. From up on the third floor he heard

Miss Alma calling for Pete. That wasn't good.

Dan ran up to find Miss Alma and tell her about the live wire touching the iron fence. He called out her name as he approached, so as not to alarm her, and told her the whole story. She told him that Pete was nowhere to be found and did not hide the fact that now she was very worried.

"Okay, let's go over our options logically," Dan said. "We've got two very sick people downstairs, and Pete is missing. We can't go anywhere near that fence and we don't have a phone to call out. But we need to try and get someone's attention, 'cause I'm pretty sure — I'm pretty sure Roger and my uncle were poisoned."

"Mercy."

Dan braced himself for what he said next. He didn't want to say it, didn't want to hear Miss Alma think it might be true. Deep inside, Dan wanted to believe that he was still suffering from the blow to his head.

"Miss Alma, it's possible we're not the only ones here in the museum."

"I was beginning to wonder that myself," she answered.

A Puzzle Solved

"Miss Alma, I have an idea," Dan said. "I think it's our best shot, and you're gonna have to trust me. If Pete's still here, it's a safe bet that he's in trouble. And one of us has to help him. It makes sense that it's me. You've looked in all the rooms, which means I've got to look other places."

They both knew Dan meant the hidden passages and staircases. Much to Dan's surprise, Miss Alma agreed. She nodded and gave him her key ring with keys that opened every door in Eckert House.

"First, though," Miss Alma instructed, "I want you to go up in the attic. Check the small windows that look out toward Filkins Street. You may be able to get someone's attention."

Before she would let Dan go, Miss Alma made him follow her to the second floor. There, in the toy room, she handed him a baseball bat and a whistle.

"I want you to blow this every minute or so, just to let me know you're all right."

Dan agreed. Miss Alma said she was going to try and do something to help Dan's uncle and Roger. Just exactly what, she wasn't sure. If they were poisoned in some way, it was going to be tricky.

"No, it's not!" exclaimed Dan suddenly. He remembered something he had read while earning a first aid badge in Boy Scouts a few years ago. "Do we have a medical kit of some kind here in the museum?"

Miss Alma assured him they did.

"Then give each one of them syrup of Ipecac followed by activated charcoal. The charcoal . . . well, it does something to any acids in their stomach, and the other stuff makes them throw up."

"How on earth did you — ?"

"It's something we should have done a while ago. No offense, Miss Alma, but get down there. Now."

Miss Alma hurried away. But not before giving Dan one last order. "I want to hear that whistle every minute!"

Dan raced to the steep stairs that led to the attic.

The attic of Eckert House was a large space that covered the main part of the house but did not spill over into the north and south wings. Those parts of the building had their own attic spaces. The ceiling was the underside of the sloping roof, but unlike other attics in smaller houses, there was no need to bend over. It was roomy. Even a tall man could stand up straight and not hit his head on the beams.

There were a number of small rooms in the attic. This is where the servants had lived so many years ago. These rooms were now filled with boxes and crates, which contained items collected by the Eckerts that were not on display downstairs. It was in one of these boxes that Rick Doheny had uncovered the Chinese puzzle box.

The rain pounded loudly over Dan's head as he made his way to the south end of the attic. The peak of the roof there was higher than the south wing, and there were two small, fan-shaped windows on either side of the chimney. Dan had little hope that anyone down along Filkins Street would be able to see him.

The rain was coming down so hard that Dan could not even see the next house. It was only half a block away. No one would ever see his dim flashlight, no matter how many SOS's he sent. Even so, he knelt before each window and flashed the emergency signal several times.

"So much for that," he said, next raising the whistle to his lips. The sound was so loud and shrill it hurt Dan's ears. He had no doubt that Miss Alma could hear it in the house far below.

Dan now had a choice. There were three concealed passageways that wound up and down through the main part of the house. All of them were built around the three chimneys that rose from the center, the north, and the south ends of the original house. Dan was at the south end, and he pushed on the secret panel next to the brick. The door opened, and Dan stepped into the darkness. He stood very still, listening for the sound of some kind of movement below. He heard nothing.

"Pete?" he called out. "Pete, are you there?" There was no answer. He shone his flashlight down the twisted steps and called out again. Something in Dan's gut told him to move on, that this was a dead end.

Dan blew the whistle again.

The center passageway wound round the large main chimney. Dan stepped into this one and quickly descended to the main floor. He called Pete's name, listened, then blew the whistle as he opened the secret door around the side of the large fireplace in the Main Salon. Then he returned to the attic.

That left the passageway that hugged the north chimney. Dan never got there.

As Dan crossed the attic, he heard a noise to his right. He spun and shone his flashlight toward the spot. He half expected to see a rat, but what he saw was an opening in the wall. It was no more than a small crack, maybe four feet high, but it was not one he had ever seen before.

Was there another way down?

"Hello?" he said aloud. "Pete?"

Dan knelt, wedged his fingers into the opening, and pulled. It was a door. It swung open. His flashlight revealed not a narrow staircase winding down to the lower parts of the house, but a crude kind of ladder nailed right into the wall.

"Pete?" Dan called again.

From far below Dan thought he heard a moan.

"Pete? It's Dan! Are you down there?"

Dan knew that if he went down the ladder, he would not be able to take the baseball bat with him. That would leave him without any way to defend himself should he need it. But if Pete were down there?

"It's not like you have a choice, Pruitt," he muttered. He laid the bat down, tucked the flashlight into his belt, swung his leg over the edge of the floor, and began to climb down the ladder. Before he did, he blew the whistle again.

The climb down was easy; the rungs were nailed to the wall every two feet. As he went deeper, Dan thought that this might be the space where he had found the drawing of Kilroy.

He was right and he was wrong. The ladder ended at the third floor, and for a minute Dan thought he was going to have to climb back up. He shone the light around and realized there were hinges on the floor.

"Only one reason for those," he said. He got on his hands and knees, felt around for some place to wedge his fingers, found what looked like a gap in the boards, and pulled. A trap door opened. Below him was the space behind the wall on the second floor that he had explored two days ago. Unfortunately there was no ladder to get down.

Just then Dan heard a sound further below. Was that another moan? "Pete! Is that you?" he called.

Dan leaned over the edge and peered down into the darkness. The beam of the flashlight didn't show much, but the floor did look like it was solid enough. If he dropped down, he didn't think he would fall through to the first floor.

"And how are you going to get back up?" he asked himself. He'd have to worry about that later. Pete might be down there — and badly hurt.

He tucked the flashlight into his pants, then he eased himself over the edge. When his arms were fully extended, he let go.

Dan hit the floor with a thud but didn't fall over.

"Pete?" he called out. There was no answer.

Dan pulled the flashlight out and proceeded down the narrow space between the walls. He found the picture of Kilroy a few moments later.

He stopped at the spot where the panel opened into the room with the toy exhibit and looked for some kind of release. He didn't find one.

Dan walked on. The passageway came to a T-intersection.

To the right was the back wall of the mansion and another ladder that had to lead down to the first floor.

To the left and down about fifteen feet or so, the passageway took another turn.

Dan stepped to the left.

"Wrong," said a voice from behind him. "You want to come this way, dude."

Dan froze, unable to move. It was Rick Doheny.

In a flash Rick had his hand over Dan's mouth. He twisted Dan's arm behind his back and dragged him to a small room off the passageway.

Dan struggled, but he was no match for Rick. Rick had Dan bound and gagged very quickly. Then Rick took the whistle from around Dan's neck.

"You haven't been keeping up, dude," he said with a smile. Then he blew the whistle. "Remind me to do that every minute or so. We don't want the Old Bag to think you're in trouble."

Rick lit a small lantern, and Dan looked around the room for some sign of Pete. He was not there. What Dan did see surprised him. The Chinese puzzle box and the dollhouse were both on a table. The puzzle box was together, but the dollhouse was apart. Each of the rooms, as Shelby had guessed, could be slid out. The frame of the dollhouse looked like a dresser with all of its drawers gone.

There were also several cages filled with rats. Some of them were white.

Even though Dan was gagged, he tried to ask about Pete. Rick understood what he was trying to say.

"Don't know where he is. Don't care," Rick answered.

Dan wanted to believe him. Could Pete have somehow gotten out of Eckert House? Then a sickening thought occurred to Dan.

What if Pete was trapped beneath the large branch out front? After all, Chester was waiting there. It was almost as if he was guarding something.

"Now listen very carefully, dude," Rick said. "You've messed me up for the last time."

There was a wild look in Rick's eyes. He was unshaven, and his hair was long and shaggy. He wore a shirt that matched the piece of fabric Dan had found on his fence.

"Since you're here, you might as well make yourself useful." Rick was making loops and tying complicated knots on a long rope as he talked. "You really don't know when to quit, do you, Danny Boy?"

Rick blew the whistle again.

"All's well." He chuckled. "In a way, this is better. Every time she hears this whistle, she thinks you're fine. And she's a little busy with your uncle and his buddy. Thanks to me."

So Uncle Jeff was right, Dan thought. They were poisoned. He looked around the room for some sign of what Rick had used so that when he escaped he could—

Dan stopped. There was a very real possibility that there would be no escape this time.

Rick finished what he was doing with the rope, slipped it around Dan's neck, wound it around his wrists and then around his left knee. When he was done, he undid the rope with which he had originally tied Dan. Dan's hands were now loose enough to move around, but Rick held the other end of the rope. Dan guessed that if he made any sudden moves Rick was prepared to deal with him. A minute had gone by, and Rick blew the whistle again.

"Okay, dude, now here's the deal," Rick explained. "I need your help. I'm gonna give you a few basic instructions. If you don't do exactly as I say . . ." Rick pulled tightly on the rope. The pain around Dan's neck was intense. So was the pain in his knee. He fell to the ground as if he had been kicked from behind. He gasped for air. "Is that clear?" asked Rick.

It was. Dan nodded Rick eased up on the rope, and Dan struggled to his feet. Rick went over to the table and began rearranging the loose pieces of the dollhouse. As he did, he talked to Dan, and Dan finally understood the events of the past few days.

"You dudes were pretty sharp. You figured out that this dollhouse was the second puzzle box. I missed that."

Dan pictured Rick on the other side of the wall, listening to everything Dan, Pete, and Shelby had said.

"Of course you missed some stuff you shouldn't have." Rick took the old piece of paper from the hidden compartment inside the pagoda and read from it. "'A little touch, seeker within a larger touch, seeker.' Could it have been more obvious?"

Dan shook his head, confused.

"The letters in the words 'touch, seeker' are just the letters in 'Eckert House' all jumbled up. A little Eckert House within a larger Eckert House. Duplicate walls? Get it? The dollhouse, dude. That's the little Eckert House within the larger one. The treasure is inside it. We just have to put the rooms of the dollhouse back in the right order and it's mine."

That's where Dan came in. Solving the puzzle required two people. Rick had tried unsuccessfully on his own.

Rick explained what he wanted Dan to do. "And just in case you get any ideas . . ." Rick pulled on the rope again. Dan fell to the ground in pain.

With his hands somewhat loose, Dan was able to take the first miniature dollhouse room that Rick handed him and hold it in place. He soon saw why it would take two people to solve the puzzle. After the first room was slid into its slot, it would pop back out when the second room was inserted. It was all controlled by some mechanism inside. According to Rick, the rooms needed to be inserted in the correct order—and held in place—to find the treasure. If the rooms were inserted and stayed in without popping out, then the puzzle was not being solved properly. That was how the secret was protected for so many years.

"I thought about smashing this lousy thing to bits, dude, but I might destroy the treasure in the process. I think I know what the treasure is and where it is, but if I'm wrong . . ."

Dan struggled to hold the pieces in, but his hands slipped a couple of times and they had to start over.

Rick was not pleased and gave the rope a slight tug each time. It hurt Dan but did not jerk him to the floor.

Finally, the fourth time they attempted to put it together, it worked. When all the rooms were in place, a drawer popped open next to the dollhouse parlor. Inside, wrapped in a piece of silk, was a small book about the size of a deck of cards. It looked very old.

Rick burst out laughing. "I was right, dude! I was right!"

A
DANGEROUS
RISK

The object inside the dollhouse was a
Bible. It was hand-written, in Chinese,
and illustrated with tiny but detailed little
pictures. According to Rick it dated back
to the late–1200s and was a gift from
Kublai Khan to Marco Polo. Marco Polo
had presented Kublai Khan with a copy
of the Holy Scriptures in Latin, and out
of respect, Kublai Khan had them
translated. Rick had believed the
rumors that Julius Eckert brought it
back from China.

"Do you know how much this is worth, dude? Millions! It's 'a treasure of the greatest worth' just like the clue promised!"

Just to be near something that old and that valuable affected Dan, and for a moment he forgot the danger he was in and edged closer to the book. Rick was studying it in the weak light of the lamp. In the excitement of the moment, both seemed to forget that Dan was Rick's prisoner.

"This is history, dude. This is the real deal." Rick sounded like his old self, like the easy-going slacker who had treated Dan like a buddy only a few short weeks ago. "We're the only ones who know it's here." Then he paused. "Help me, dude. Help me and I'll give you a piece of the action."

In that moment, in that split second, Dan knew that his fears about being like Rick Doheny were groundless. Dan may have made plenty of mistakes and gotten himself into difficult situations, but the difference between them was that in those same circumstances, Rick blamed others while Dan blamed himself. Dan looked to God for forgiveness and guidance. Rick didn't think forgiveness was needed, just help to get away with even more.

Dan was still gagged, and he made a sound and indicated his mouth with his hands. Rick loosened the gag.

"What did you have in mind?" Dan asked, stalling for time. He moved his head around as if his neck was sore. What he was really doing, though, was making a mental note of everything in the room.

"Five hundred thousand dollars," Rick answered.

Dan nodded. He knew he had one shot at freedom. A moment later, he took it.

Rick loosened his grip on the rope. Dan laced his fingers together into a large fist and swung for Rick's head. Rick went down. Dan then swept everything off the table — including the lamp. The room was plunged into darkness, but Dan knew what he was doing and where he was going. He picked up the Bible and made a break for it.

When Rick brought Dan into the room earlier, Dan had glanced over at the space against the back wall of the house and the ladder that went down into the darkness. That's where Dan headed now, grabbing the flashlight and pulling off the rope as he went. Dan knew the ladder would be difficult to climb down, but that meant it would also be difficult for Rick to follow.

Dan had a good sense of direction and he calculated that he was right above the kitchen. He was, but after descending a good thirty feet or so he realized that there was no exit into that part of the house. The passageway continued its drop below him. He risked a quick look with the flashlight. It was not strong enough to reach the bottom of the hole, but the ladder continued down. Dan flipped off the light, trusted his footing, and climbed down it as quickly as he could.

"You're not going anywhere, partner," Rick hollered from above. He had obviously recovered. "There's no way out."

"Sorry, partner," Dan shouted back. "I don't believe you."

A heavy object came hurtling down at Dan in the dark. It was a large tray of some kind. It clanged against the wall and made so much noise coming down that Dan was able to avoid it.

There were two basements in Eckert House, one below the other. By the time Dan reached the bottom of the ladder, he realized he was further down than even the lowest basement. Something else came crashing down the shaft toward Dan.

"You missed," Dan yelled.

"Guess who I'm not gonna miss?" Rick taunted. "All your friends are just sitting up here. I can get them, and they won't even know what happened."

Dan had to act fast—before Rick killed them all. Dan pulled the ancient book from his pocket.

"Hey, Rick," he called out, "guess what I have? I'll give you a clue. It's worth millions of dollars, and only two people know it exists."

"Thief!" yelled Rick.

"Now you've gone and hurt my feelings," Dan answered.

He had to get Rick away from the others. But how? Then his fingers found a loose piece of paper tucked inside the cover of the book.

"Hey, partner, guess what I'm doing now." Dan tore the piece of paper slowly in half.

"No!" Rick screamed.

"Hey, that was fun. Let me try another one." Dan ripped the same page in half. "I wonder how much I just cost you?"

Rick could be heard hurrying down the ladder. Dan reached the bottom, and his foot brushed up against the tray. Thinking it might come in handy, as a shield at the very least, he picked it up.

Just to make sure Rick wouldn't change his mind about following him, Dan took out the paper again.

"Marco!" Dan called out. He ripped the page into quarters. "Hey, Rick, you're supposed to say 'Polo.' You never played that game? Marco!" Dan made another noisy rip.

Once in the passage, Dan turned his flashlight on again. He was in a stone tunnel. It sloped down at a gentle angle, and there were no obstructions. He turned the light off and moved as quickly as he could through the pitch black. He hadn't gone fifty feet when he heard Rick enter the tunnel behind him.

"Marco," Rick called out. He was laughing.

"Hey, Rick, did you see that I left part of the book back there in the corner?" This wasn't true, but Dan hoped Rick would take some time and actually look. He needed every second he could get.

Did Rick pause and look back? Dan thought so, and he risked another look forward with his flashlight. The tunnel remained clear for the next twenty feet or so. Dan's best guess was that he was already under the stone wall that circled the house.

Dan felt cooler air rushing up toward him, and instinct told him to stop. He was glad he did, for his next step might have been his last. A quick look with his flashlight revealed the steepest flight of stone steps Dan had ever seen.

"Boo," said Rick quietly. He was *ten feet* behind Dan!

Dan looked ahead. He knew what he had to do.

In one swift motion, Dan set the tray on the ground, pushed it over the edge of the top step, jumped on, leaned forward, and launched himself down the stone staircase.

In theory, this was no different than some of the tricks Dan pulled with his skateboard on the cement steps and handrails all over Freemont. Balance, pitch, and guts were all part of the game. But this was no game. His flashlight barely allowed him to see where he was going, and he had no idea what was waiting for him in the darkness below.

Focus, Pruitt, he told himself. Then, unable to ignore the insanity of what he was doing he said, "I can't believe this is what you had in mind when you said 'deeper,' God."

The ride was intense, but Dan made it to the bottom of the stone steps in one piece. Just how steep a drop it was, he hadn't a clue. He only knew it felt like he'd made a lightning-fast trip to the bottom of the Grand Canyon. He had put a lot of distance between himself and Rick, but now he had to keep it.

This tunnel has to go somewhere, he thought, *and I've got to get there fast*. He kept his flashlight on and ran forward. He figured he had to be below the park across the street from Eckert House. This part of the tunnel had about four inches of water in it, which would make sense if he were that close to the river. But where did it come out?

Another set of stone steps rose out of the darkness. They climbed at just as steep an angle as the ones behind Dan.

The sound of water splashing told Dan that Rick had made it down the steps and was running toward him.

Carrying the tray was now impossible because Dan needed both of his hands to climb the steps. He reluctantly tossed it aside.

It was cold and wet in the tunnel, but Dan was sweating and his breathing was labored. His head was pounding, too, and he knew he wasn't going as fast as he could have if he were fully recovered.

Rick was now on the steps below him.

Where did this come out? Dan wondered.

Please, God was his simple prayer.

Rick was closer now.

The stairs ended at a stone door. There was no handle. Dan pushed on it with all of his strength. It didn't move.

"Marco!" Rick yelled as he hurled himself at Dan.

The force of Rick's body hitting Dan's body jarred the door at Dan's back. It shoved open, and they tumbled out into the rain. Dan rolled over and looked up. They were at the base of the war memorial.

Their sudden exit stunned Rick, and Dan used those seconds to twist out of his grasp. Dan scrambled to his feet and ran toward Eckert House. In the back of his mind was a vague plan to get Rick near the deadly fence, an action that Dan was aware could backfire and result in his own injury. Rick regained his footing, tackled Dan, flipped him on his back, and pinned him to the ground.

"Where's the Bible?" Rick panted.

"Back there," Dan yelled, "getting soaked in the rain!" The book was actually still safe in the back pocket of his jeans. Rick pressed his knee against Dan's chest. The pain was intense.

Rick looked over his shoulder to check and lifted his knee as he did. It was enough for Dan to roll away, and he got to his feet before Rick's arm was around his neck again. Rick threw Dan on his back.

"This is over," Rick yelled, panting. He was right, but not for the reason he thought. Several figures emerged from the heavy rain. One of them, a man, tackled Rick, and they tumbled away from Dan.

Dan thought the man looked familiar, but he didn't see how it was possible for him to be here. Moments later Dan saw that it *was* Agent Havens, the man from the FBI who had been tracking Rick Doheny. Rick was no match for him. Agent Havens had Rick handcuffed and subdued in a matter of seconds.

"You have the right to remain silent," Agent Havens said. He was interrupted. Mrs. Doheny was one of the other people who had come running up.

"But you won't," she said to Rick. She looked furious. "You're going to tell the police and the FBI and the CIA and anybody who asks you a question, anything they want to know. Is that understood? Is it?"

Rick scowled, and Agent Havens finished reading him his rights. Dan's mother and his cousin Pete came up and hugged Dan tight. Dan leaned against them gratefully. "Where'd you guys come from?"

His mom pulled Dan under the shelter of a tree, then explained. Mrs. Doheny knew Rick was back in Freemont. She knew it because when Miss Alma surprised Dan in Rick's room, Dan dropped the piece of fabric he had brought with him. Mrs. Doheny found it, recognized it, realized Dan was acting strange for a reason, put two and two together, got four, and waited for Rick. She knew he would return to Eckert House, so she spent almost forty-eight hours parked in her car near the museum waiting for her son.

Dan had a lot of respect for Mrs. Doheny.

"Which is exactly as it should be," snapped Miss Alma the next day when they were sorting out all that had happened. "Does she sometimes ramble on and on? No question. Does she make the worst pies in Freemont? Ask anyone. Is she a fool?" Miss Alma snorted. "Ask Rick."

There was a logical explanation for the others being in the park as well. Pete had escaped Eckert House before the wire fell on the fence and trapped everyone inside. He had surprised Rick on the second floor and barely made it to the front door ahead of him. Pete managed to get home and get through to Dan's mother. She called the FBI and Agent Havens hurried to Freemont. They were trying to figure out a way to get into Eckert House without getting electrocuted when Mrs. Doheny saw Rick and Dan pop out of the monument. They got to Dan just in time.

Pete's father and Roger were fine. Rick had put poison in the security office coffeemaker. Dan's idea about the Ipecac and charcoal the got them out of danger.

"Not a pleasant hour," said Shelby with a shudder.

The doctor said he'd be willing to write Dan a recommendation to medical school.

Sorting out the mystery of the Chinese puzzle box and the Bible that was concealed within the doll-house was a little more complicated. Miss Alma could not believe she had missed the fact that the pagoda and the dollhouse were a matched set.

The Bible was not from the 1200s. It was valuable, but worth only thousands, not the millions Rick had claimed. It was hand written, and the illustrations were quite beautiful, but research revealed that a Chinese student who was studying with a missionary in Beijing created it in the mid–1800s.

"It's hardly a 'treasure of greatest worth,'" concluded Dan. "Back in 1875 it would have been worth even less."

Miss Alma looked quite annoyed by this statement. "Once again, Mr. Pruitt, you have stunningly missed the point."

"Okay," Dan responded, knowing she would tell him how.

"What is it?" she demanded. "Define the object you see." The Bible was being carefully repaired in the workroom on the third floor. Pete and Shelby were there with them.

"Well," he began, "It's a book. It's old. A lot of effort went into making it. It . . ." Dan stopped. His eyes fell on one of the tiny illustrations. Abraham was climbing a mountain with his son Isaac. Isaac didn't know it, but Abraham was about to sacrifice him. Abraham didn't know it, but God was not going to allow that to happen. It was all a test, helping Abraham's relationship with God to grow deeper.

Deeper.

Abraham listened and did what he was told.

Deeper.

Listening was what it was all about. And then obeying, of course. Listening didn't count for much if you didn't follow up on it.

"It's the Word of God," Dan finally said. "It's one of the ways he talks to us. Not only us, but also to everyone who's gone before us, and everyone who will come after." Dan paused. "I guess that qualifies it as a treasure of greatest worth."

"I guess it does," Miss Alma agreed.

On their way out of the museum that afternoon, Dan, Pete, and Shelby met Will Stoller as he was coming in. The Eenies were with him.

"We're going, too! We're going, too!" they yelled.

"This is not a sporting arena," said Miss Alma sternly. "Keep your voices down."

"Going where?" asked Dan.

"To the Old Geezers Convention," they answered.

"Will Stoller!" Miss Alma said, shocked.

Will chuckled. "Well, that's what it is, in a way."

The Old Geezers Convention turned out to be the annual meeting of those veterans who flew for the Army Air Force in World War Two. It was being held in Washington D.C. in three weeks. Will was quite taken by the diary Miss Alma had given Dan, and he was doing everything he could to help Dan figure out who wrote it. Will thought the convention would be a good place to continue the investigation, so all of them—Dan, Pete, Shelby, Will, Miss Alma, and the Eenies—were going to make the trip.

"You know, Miss Alma," Will said as they walked up the stairs, "my cousin and his wife took their honeymoon trip to Washington."

"Did they?" Miss Alma answered coolly.

"What do you think?" Will asked.

"What do I think about what, Mr. Stoller?"

"Washington as a spot for a honeymoon?"

"I think it's a lovely idea. Send me a postcard when you get there."

What is  SOUL GEAR?

Based on Luke 2:52:
"And Jesus grew in wisdom and stature,
and in favor with God and men (NIV)."

2:52 is designed just for boys 8-12!
This verse is one of the only verses in
the Bible that provides a glimpse of Jesus
as a young boy. Who doesn't wonder what
Jesus was like as a kid?

Become smarter, stronger, deeper,
and cooler as you develop
into a young man of God
with 2:52 Soul Gear™!

Zonder**kidz**

The 2:52 Soul Gear™ takes a closer look by focusing on the four major areas of development highlighted in Luke 2:52:

"Wisdom" = mental/emotional = **Smarter**

"Stature" = physical = **Stronger**

"Favor with God" = spiritual = **Deeper**

"Favor with men" = social = **Cooler**

2:52 Mysteries of Eckert House

Three friends seek to uncover the hidden mysteries of Eckert House in this four-book series filled with adventure, mystery, and intrigue.

2:52 Mysteries of Eckert House: Hidden in Plain Sight [Book 1]

Written by Chris Auer
Eerie stories surround the old Victorian mansion-turned-museum known as Eckert House. But what was once thought to be fiction may prove to be fact after twelve-year-old Dan Pruitt makes a gruesome discovery.
Sofcover 0-310-70870-2

2:52 Mysteries of Eckert House: A Stranger, a Thief & a Pack of Lies [Book 2]

Written by Chris Auer
Many secrets lie within the walls of Eckert House, but no one is prepared when a stranger, claiming to be the sole heir of Eckert House, shows up.
Sofcover 0-310-70871-0

2:52 Mysteries of Eckert House: The Forgotten Room [Book 4]

Written by Chris Auer
Dan Pruitt's certain he's found a hidden room. But when he and his friends set out to find it, they uncover more than a room. What they find will ultimately lead to danger; how will they keep their secret safe and protect themselves too?
Softcover 0-310-70873-7

Available now at your local bookstore!

Zonderkidz.

The 2:52 Boys Bible–
the "ultimate manual" for boys

The 2:52 Boys Bible, NIV
Features written by Rick Osborne

Become more like Jesus mentally, physically, spiritually, and socially–Smarter, Stronger, Deeper, and Cooler—with the *2:52 Boys Bible!*

Hardcover 0-310-70320-4
Softcover 0-310-70552-5

Also from Inspirio . . .

CD Holder   ISBN: 0-310-99033-5

Book & Bible Holder

Med   ISBN: 0-310-98823-3

Large ISBN: 0-310-98824-1

inspirio
The gift group of Zondervan

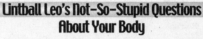

We want to hear from you. Please send your comments about this
book to us in care of zreview@zondervan.com. Thank you.

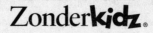

Grand Rapids, MI 49530
www.zonderkidz.com